FOR FINNUR
x x x

First published 2022 by Two Hoots
This edition published 2023 by Two Hoots
an imprint of Pan Macmillan
The Smithson, 6 Briset Street London EC1M 5NR
EU representative: Macmillan Publishers Ireland Limited, 1st Floor,
The Liffey Trust Centre, 117-126 Sheriff Street Upper, Dublin 1, D01 YC43
Associated companies throughout the world
www.panmacmillan.com

ISBN: 978-1-5290-2614-6

1 3 5 7 9 8 6 4 2

A CIP catalogue record for this book is available from the British Library.
Printed in China
The illustrations in this book were painted in gouache and then digitally coloured.

www.twohootsbooks.com

book belongs to

. . . .

MORAG HOOD

TEAPOT TROUBLE

A DUCK AND TINY HORSE ADVENTURE

TW🦉 HOOTS

Something strange had
happened to Duck's teapot,

and Duck was not impressed.

"Out of my way!"

said Tiny Horse.

"For I am the greatest
at solving teapot disasters
and I will save the day!"

But it wasn't as easy as that.

"MYSTERIOUS POINTY BEAST!" said Tiny Horse. "I shall defeat you."

"I think it's a crab,"
said Duck.

"**AH-HA!**"

said Tiny Horse.
"I once worked in a
crab-taming shop."

"I know exactly how
to deal with this."

"No crab can resist a lovely picnic," said Tiny Horse. "It will definitely come out now."

But the picnic was not a great success.

"The food must not have been nice enough,"
said Tiny Horse.

Tiny Horse's other ideas did not
tempt the crab either.

CELERY!

MAGNIFICENT HAT!

MYSTERY BOX!

TRAMPOLINE!

FLOWERS!

PEAS!

Duck didn't think he would
ever get his teapot back.

Until—

"I have solved the problem entirely!"
said Tiny Horse.

"I have made you a new teapot so
everything is totally fine now."

"TA - DAH!" said Tiny Horse.

"THAT IS ABSOLUTELY <u>NOT</u> A TEAPOT.

Have you ever even seen a teapot?" said Duck.
"Or a crab? You don't know anything
about anything."

"**NEVER FEAR!**"

said Tiny Horse.

"For I have a brand-new
greatest idea ever!"

But Duck wasn't interested.

"I am going out," he said.
"And I am taking my
teapot with me."

"Where are you going?" said Tiny Horse.

"This is no way to find a new teapot."

"What are you even
doing here?"

"I'm collecting shells,"
said Duck . . .

"...for our little crab friend."

"A shell won't work as a teapot!" said Tiny Horse.

"Whoever heard of something so ridiculous?"

But finally Duck was reunited with
the only teapot he had ever wanted.

And the crab . . .

. . . moved into his new home.

"You're welcome,"
said Tiny Horse.

How to draw a
MYSTERIOUS POINTY BEAST

Start by drawing an egg.

Add some pointy claws.

Draw two lollipop shapes,

and some legs.

Give your beast a mouth and two dots for the eyes . . .

TA-DAH!